TWO of a kind™
Diaries

Look for more

titles:

TWO of a kind™ Diaries

P.S. Wish You Were Here

by Megan Stine
from the series created by
Robert Griffard & Howard Adler

HarperEntertainment
An Imprint of HarperCollinsPublishers
A PARACHUTE PRESS BOOK

A PARACHUTE PRESS BOOK

Parachute Publishing, L.L.C.
156 Fifth Avenue
Suite 302
New York, NY 10010

Published by
HarperEntertainment

An Imprint of HarperCollins*Publishers*
10 East 53rd Street, New York, NY 10022-5299

TWO OF A KIND books created and produced by Parachute Press, L.L.C., in cooperation with Dualstar Publications, a division of Dualstar Entertainment Group, Inc., published by HarperEntertainment, an imprint of HarperCollins*Publishers*.

For information address HarperCollins Publishers Inc., 10 East 53rd Street, New York, NY 10022-5299.

ISBN 0-06-106581-1

HarperCollins®, ®, and HarperEntertainment™ are trademarks of HarperCollins Publishers Inc.

First printing: June 2000

Printed in the United States of America

Visit HarperEntertainment on the World Wide Web at
www.harpercollins.com

10 9 8 7 6 5 4

Chapter 1

Saturday

Dear Diary,

This is so weird. I can't believe I'm sitting here in my room at White Oak Academy all alone. And I mean *totally* alone. Phoebe, my roommate, is downstairs working on a poetry project with a friend. All the other girls are hanging out in the student lounge. Or else they're at the library, pretending to study.

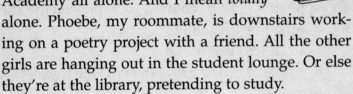

So that leaves me. Just me.

WITHOUT MARY-KATE!!

Yup. That's the big news, Diary. Mary-Kate left an hour ago. Can you believe it? She went back home! Dad came to get her, and they flew back to Chicago. She's going to spend the rest of the year at our old school, with all her friends.

Good-bye, Mary Kate!

So here I am, moping around Porter House. In the middle of New Hampshire.

Without my twin sister.

As I watched Mary-Kate and Dad get in the car to go to the airport, my stomach did a flip-flop. How could Mary-Kate leave me here? I asked myself. We'd never been apart for more than one night. *Ever*.

But Mary-Kate really missed her old friends—and especially her softball team—back home.

Besides, I guess I deserved it, after what I did to her. Writing about my own sister in the White Oak newspaper's gossip column wasn't exactly the *nicest* thing I've ever done.

In fact, it was pretty slimy.

On a scale of one to ten, with ten as the slimiest . . .

Okay—ten.

What was I thinking, Diary? No, wait. Don't answer that! You know all my secrets. So you *know* what I was thinking! I hate to admit it, but I guess I thought I'd be more popular if I put some really juicy stuff in my column.

Like telling the whole world who Mary-Kate had a crush on.

But I changed my mind. Remember, Diary? I didn't *mean* for that article to get published. I wrote another column and asked Dana Woletsky, the editor, to use it instead. But Dana printed the first version anyway. It was all a big mistake!

Make that *huge*.

"You know I'm sorry," I told Mary-Kate as she hoisted her suitcase into the trunk of the car. "I never meant for things to turn out like that."

"I know," Mary-Kate said, tucking a strand of blond hair behind her ear. "Let's not talk about it anymore, okay?"

I could see from the look in her eyes that she was trying to forgive me. We had even sort of made up. The two of us were acting perfectly nice to each other.

But Mary-Kate was still leaving.

She finished packing her trunk. Then she hopped into the car with Dad and drove away.

For half a second, I wanted to run after the car, yelling, "Wait! I'll come home with you!"

But the truth is, I love being here at White Oak Academy.

So I just watched the car disappear through the trees. Then I hurried back into Porter House, shivering. Even though it's April, it's still pretty cool out.

"Anyone want to make hot chocolate with me?" I asked, poking my head into the lounge.

No one answered.

"I've got marshmallows," I tried to tempt everyone.

No answer. Alyssa and Wendy were busy playing a video game. Phoebe smiled at me, then went back to her poetry book. And Kristin is on a diet. She just rolled her eyes at me.

So I made myself a mug of cocoa and trudged up to my room.

What am I going to do without Mary-Kate, Diary?

I guess I'll find out soon enough. I mean, it's not as if I'm miserable. I love White Oak Academy. And even if Mary-Kate *is* gone, I still have my roommate, Phoebe. She and I are going to write a column for the school newspaper.

(It's not a gossip column this time, though. It's a fashion column. Won't that be weird? I mean, Phoebe is nice, but she's *still* wearing those old vintage clothes. Last week she bought an old wool coat with a fur collar. It's shedding worse than a cat. I'm thinking of feeding it!)

Anyway, I also have good old cousin Jeremy, at the Harrington School next door. So at least my link to the world of boys is intact!

(Speaking of boys—Yikes! I have to E-mail my boyfriend, Ross Lambert. I haven't talked to him for five whole days. I've just been so busy!)

But back to the big problem, Diary. I'll be okay without Mary-Kate—won't I?

My stomach just did another flip-flop.

P.S. Wish You Were Here

Straighten up, Ashley. Stop worrying about Mary-Kate. She's gone. And you're on your own now.

Besides, we promised to call each other. And E-mail. So we won't be totally out of touch.

And I hate to bring this up, but I just noticed my homework schedule. It's posted on my bulletin board. I've got a book report due for Ms. Bloomberg's English class in just a few days. And I'm determined to stay on her good side—she actually liked my last paper.

I've already read the book. I picked *The Old Man and the Sea*. Now all I have to do is start writing my report.

The Old Man, the Sea, and the Very Big Fish

Did I say *all* I have to do?

Reality check! Ms. Bloomberg said our papers have to be at least five pages long, with no spelling errors or typos. We need a strong theme. And we have to fully explain where the turning point in the story is.

Yikes!

Gotta run, Diary. I'd better get busy right now!

Chapter 2

Sunday

Dear Diary,

Well, I did it. Yesterday, I came back  to Chicago. It sure was weird flying home from White Oak without Ashley. Just me and Dad on the plane, the whole way. Talk about a long trip!

Dad tried to make conversation, but I wasn't really listening.

"So how about those Cubs?" he asked me.

Dad knows I'm totally into sports. I'm a die-hard Chicago fan. Cubs. Bears. Bulls. You name it. If it's an animal, and it plays any kind of ball for Chicago, I'm there.

"They lost their last game," I muttered, staring out the window at the clouds.

"Yeah, but only because the umpire was blind," Dad said.

"Blind?" I said, frowning. "Doesn't that disqualify him as a umpire?"

Dad stared at me. "It's just an expression," he said.

"Oh." I was still only half listening. "Right."

"Mary-Kate, is there anything you want to tell

me?" Dad asked. He sounded really concerned.

I shook my head.

How could I tell him what was on my mind?

That Ashley and I had had a major fight. And that we still weren't on the very best of terms.

Here's the truth: One of the reasons I left White Oak was because of what Ashley did.

But I couldn't tell Dad that. Not without ratting on her. And making Ashley sound like the selfish traitor that she is!

Okay, I'm going too far.

But Ashley really hurt me when she wrote about me in the *Acorn*'s gossip column. What am I supposed to do? Send her a thank-you note?

I guess I'm still pretty upset—even though she did apologize. I mean, she's definitely sorry. And I know it was an accident. She's not really that kind of person, Diary. Not deep down.

So I think I've forgiven her.

But I'm not sure—will I ever be able to trust Ashley again?

That's what I kept wondering on the plane.

Anyhow, it probably won't be long before Ashley calls. We promised each other we'd talk on the phone right away. I'll let her call me first.

When Dad and I finally got back to the house,

my whole mood changed. It was *fantastic* to be home.

"Mary-Kate!" Carrie yelled, running to the door. She gave me a giant hug. Carrie Moore's our baby-sitter, and she's the best ever. She takes care of Ashley and me (now just me!) while Dad is teaching his college classes. "Are we on for some house hockey, or what?" Carrie asked.

Dad flinched. "House hockey?" he asked weakly. His eyes scanned the room, checking out the breakables.

"Oh, no," Carrie covered up. "Did I say house hockey? I meant house*cleaning*. Yeah. What do you say, Mary-Kate? You take the bathroom, I'll do the den. We'll rock this place clean!"

I laughed. Dad rolled his eyes. He knew she was kidding. Carrie helped me lug my bags up to my room. She's still the best. I really missed her while I was at White Oak Academy. She is absolutely the coolest twenty-six-year-old I've ever known.

Anyway, having Carrie around made me feel like I wasn't so alone anymore. And that cheered me up.

Okay, I decided. It's time for me to find out what it's like to live without Ashley.

Besides, I'm not really going to be alone at all.

I HAVE MY OLD FRIENDS BACK! YES!!

P.S. Wish You Were Here

Right after Carrie helped me unpack, Max and Brian came over. And of course we talked about our neighborhood softball team, the Belmont Bashers. That was another reason I decided to come home in the middle of the school year. To help the team win.

"All right! The babe of the Belmont Bashers is back!" Max said, slapping me five.

The three of us flopped down in the living room. "So have things been getting better for you guys?" I asked. The team had been on a serious losing streak lately.

"We need you, Mary-Kate," Brian moaned. "We're down four games. The Sherwood Aces trashed us last week."

"No way," I said. I grabbed an apple from the fruit bowl on the coffee table. Then I gripped it like a softball and tossed it to Max.

He missed and the apple landed on the carpet. I guess the guys *did* need my help!

"They've got a pitcher who can throw a sinker," Max said.

"But now we've got a batter who can hit one!" Brian replied, pointing at me.

"Right," I said. But inside, I felt my stomach drop.

Hit a sinker? I wasn't so sure about that. I mean, I'd been staying in pretty good shape practicing with the Mighty Oaks. Sort of. I had to work really hard just to get on that team.

But no one on the White Oak team, even my roommate, Campbell Smith, had a prayer of pitching a sinker ball. So I had no clue if I could really hit one.

"Boy, are we glad to have you back," Max kept repeating.

Yeah, I thought. I'd better come through for the team. No pressure or anything. Ha!

I guess Max and Brian weren't all *that* glad to have me back, because they didn't stay long. Just long enough to eat half the brownies Carrie had baked as a welcome home treat.

After the guys left, Carrie drove me over to my friend Amanda's to spend the night. Amanda and I had the best time in the whole world. We ordered pizza and rented two movies. But we hardly watched them because we ended up talking all night. Amanda wanted to hear every single detail about White Oak Academy. I told her everything— about the houses, and all the old traditions. And how fancy the dining hall was. And all about the boys' school down the street.

P.S. Wish You Were Here

Actually, White Oak sounded better when I talked about it than it was while I was there!

"It sounds *so* cool," Amanda said. "How could you ever leave? But hey, I'm glad you did!" she added really quickly.

Why *did* I leave? I wondered. Because I missed Dad and Carrie and all my friends. And because the Belmont Bashers needed me back. But also, like I said, it was because of my fight with Ashley.

I didn't say anything about that to Amanda, though. It was too private. I mean, I'm not going to bad-mouth my sister when she's not even there to defend herself.

Anyway, I guess Amanda *had* missed me a lot. She was practically bouncing off the walls with happiness that I was home.

Me, too. What could be better than being back with your very best friends?

It was even cooler than I thought it would be.

Except . . .

Now I'm back in my old room. Getting ready to turn out the light. But there's an empty bed beside me.

It sure is weird going to sleep in this room without Ashley.

Chapter 3

Wednesday

Dear Diary,

Don't even ask why it's been three days since I wrote to you last. It's been way crazy around here!

I thought it was going to be a breeze to slip back into my old life.

Wrong!

Switching schools—twice—in the middle of the year? Not a good idea!

For one thing, when I left Chicago a few months ago, I was doing great in math. Taylor Donovan (Mr. Gorgeous-hunk-tutor) had helped me so much that when I got to White Oak, I was actually *ahead* of everyone else!

But guess what? That means my school at home is going faster than White Oak. So now I'm behind again!

Mr. Frankel made me stay after class to talk about it.

"Mary-Kate, what happened?" he asked. "You were doing so well. Now you seem to have forgotten everything."

"Amnesia?" I joked.

"How about: Be here tomorrow morning—

early—and we'll work on it," my teacher shot back.

Bummer. Now I have to get up at six o'clock A.M. to meet with Mr. Frankel at seven o'clock.

But here's the good part.

I'm not even scared! All my math fears are gone, thanks to $a^2 \times b^2 = ?$ Taylor's tutoring. I've finally realized that I can do pre-algebra. I just don't want to!

My fear of six o'clock A.M. is a whole different story.

Anyway, after I talked to Mr. Frankel, I went to softball practice. It was awesome! The whole team swarmed around me, welcoming me back. I guess they really do need me.

"Okay, listen up, Bashers," Coach Latimore told us. "If we can win three more games, we'll make it into the playoffs. And we've got our first chance this weekend."

"No problem," I said, trying to sound confident. I picked up a bat, and Jordan threw me a pitch.

Smack! I knocked that ball almost to the end of the park.

"All right!" Max cheered.

"Mary-Kate rules!" Brian and Lisa shouted.

What can I say, Diary? It was great hearing everyone cheering for me.

But you know what's really strange? Even though I'm having a great time being back home and being with my old team, I've been feeling like something's missing for the past three days. (And I don't just mean Ashley. She hasn't even called me yet, by the way!)

What I mean is, after White Oak, it seems sort of boring to do the same old stuff all the time. I guess I got used to trying new things. It was fun having new experiences at boarding school.

That's what's missing.

So today when I saw a notice up on the bulletin board at school, I got really psyched. Tryouts for the school play are coming up on Friday—and I'm actually thinking of auditioning! They're doing *Peter Pan*, the musical. Wouldn't it be amazing if I got to be Peter?

And wouldn't Ashley be surprised?

I wonder why she hasn't called me yet.

Dear Diary,

What am I going to do? Mary-Kate is still mad at me.

I know she's still mad because she hasn't called me yet—even though we said we'd call each other right away.

14

P.S. Wish You Were Here

So yesterday I broke down and called *her*. I stood in line for an hour and ten minutes to use the hall phone. When I finally got my turn, it was after five  o'clock. I expected Mary-Kate to answer, but the phone rang four times before the machine picked up.

It was Mary-Kate's voice with a new greeting.

"Hi," she said. "Leave a message for Mary-Kate, Kevin, or Carrie, and we'll call you back. Bye!"

Wow, I thought. They've cut me out of the message! It was almost like I didn't exist anymore.

My stomach did another flip-flop. Where was Mary-Kate, anyway? She was usually home by now. That really bugged me. I mean, she was out somewhere having tons of fun, while I'm standing in a stupid line, waiting forever to use the phone!

(That's the only thing I hate about boarding school. Having just one phone for the whole dorm.) Anyway, I got so flustered that when the machine beeped, I didn't know what to say. So I just said, "Hi, everyone. It's Ashley. Where are you guys? Call me back if you feel like it. Bye."

But did Mary-Kate call me back? Nope.

Now I'm seriously bummed, Diary. I mean, I

thought I'd be fine here at White Oak without her. And I probably *would* be— if she hadn't left in that "I don't need you" mood.

There's a teeny bit of good news, though. I finished my book report for Ms. Bloomberg's class! I feel pretty good about it, too.

I was in the library today at the Harrington School for Boys, doing research for my science project. My cousin Jeremy was there, so I asked him to proofread my book report for me.

"You want *me* to read it?" Jeremy asked. He sounded really surprised.

Jeremy's right, I thought. But I didn't want to hurt his feelings. So I said, "Sure. Ms. Bloomberg is a stickler for typos and grammar mistakes. And you're a good speller. Do you mind?"

Jeremy shrugged. "Why not? Hey, it gives me a good excuse to slack off on my science project."

He was sitting across from me at one of those huge library tables. All our stuff was spread out in front of us. He grabbed my book report and started reading.

"Wow," he muttered under his breath when he was halfway through. "This is good, Ashley. Really good."

"Thanks," I said. "Any spelling mistakes?"

Jeremy shook his head and kept reading.

When he was done, he just stared at me. Like I

was the Book Report Goddess or something. "This is amazing," he said. "It's the best paper I've ever read. How did you figure all this stuff out?"

"I don't know," I said. "The book was really good. So I just wrote about how it made me feel."

I reached across the table to take my paper back, but Jeremy wouldn't give it to me. He clasped it to his chest.

The Book Report Goddess

"I've got a book report due in five days," he said. "And I haven't even picked a book to read yet."

"You're kidding!" I gasped. My cousin was even more of a slacker than I thought.

Jeremy shook his head. "I am so totally behind," he moaned. "Our science projects are due Friday. I've got a huge math test to study for on Monday. And that's when my book report is due! I'm doomed."

Then Jeremy got this funny look in his eyes. Just like he always gets when he's about to spring one of his famous practical jokes.

"Wouldn't it be great if I could just turn in *your* paper, Ashley?" he said. "I mean, it's so awesome."

"Ha ha," I said. I leaned across the table and grabbed my report out of his hands. Then I glanced at it again. "Are you *sure* there aren't any

17

spelling errors? No left-out words?"

"Don't worry," Jeremy said gloomily. "You'll get an A plus. That paper's a masterpiece."

I have to admit, I felt pretty proud. Ashley Burke conquers the world!

Anyway, after that I tried to cheer Jeremy up a little about his report. I even suggested a bunch of really short books he could read.

"How about a biography of Napoleon?" I joked. "That could be *short*." Napoleon was famous for being small.

Napoleon

"How about a biography of the midget twins—Ashley and Mary-Kate Burke?" Jeremy shot back.

"Okay, smart-mouth. Let's get serious," I said. "You could read *The Pearl* by John Steinbeck. It's less than a hundred pages."

"I'm looking for something under *ten* pages," Jeremy said, sighing.

"You mean, like *Lovable Bear's Big Day*?" I teased.

Jeremy brightened. "Do you think Mr. March would accept that?"

"Uh, I doubt it," I said. "But you'll have to make the call on that one. He's *your* English teacher."

Jeremy shook his head. "No," he said finally.

"I've made up my mind. I'll just have to write my book report without reading a book."

Yikes! I guessed my cousin's English grade was headed for the toilet. But I still had tons of research to do for my science project, so I got busy. You should have seen our table. Books, papers, and notebooks were scattered everywhere.

A few minutes later my roommate, Phoebe, walked by. She was wearing a really cool, green vintage coat with big purple buttons. Not my style, really, but it looked great on her.

"Hi!" I whispered, trying to be quiet in the library.

I thought Phoebe might sit down and hang out with us. But when she saw Jeremy, she just tossed her curly brown hair and kept walking. Then she picked a different table. She doesn't really like my cousin much. Mr. Practical Joker rubs her the wrong way.

So that was my day, Diary. Not too bad—except for the part about Mary-Kate not calling me. I think I'll send her an E-mail right now. Hopefully she'll answer me. Keep your fingers crossed!

Chapter 4

Thursday

Dear Diary,

Did I say my friends were happy to have me back home?

Correction: My friends are *thrilled* to have me back—as long as I do exactly what they want me to do.

Play softball. And that's it!

If I dare mention being interested in anything else—like trying out for the school play—they *laugh* at me! And that's just what happened at lunch today.

"Did you see the poster for *Peter Pan*?" I asked Amanda. "The tryouts are tomorrow."

"So?" Amanda said, chomping into her ham and cheese sandwich.

"So I'm thinking of auditioning," I announced with a big smile.

Brian burst out laughing. Max almost spit out a mouthful of chocolate milk.

"*You*?" Brian said, his eyes wide. "Onstage?"

Amanda giggled, too. "Come on, Mary-Kate," she said. "Give us a break. You're kidding, right?"

"Why would I be kidding?" I said, frowning.

"Because," Amanda said, like it was *so* obvious.

"You're a jock, not an actress."

My face felt hot. How could my friends all *laugh* at me like that? And the worst part was, they weren't trying to hurt my feelings or anything. They *meant* it!

"Hey, Peter Pan is very athletic," I argued. "He does lots of sword fighting and flying and stuff. Besides, Peter is always played by a girl. I think it'd be the perfect part for me."

Max shook his head. "No way, Mary-Kate," he said. "I mean, what are you going to do? Dribble your way around Captain Hook? Pitch a slider to Wendy and the Lost Boys?"

Wow, I thought. They really think all I can do is play sports! That really hurt.

"Stick to softball," Brian advised me. "That's what you're good at."

"Yeah," Amanda chimed in. "You're not the actress type. You don't have a phony bone in your body."

Oh, yeah? I thought. I'm doing a pretty good job of acting right now. I'm pretending I don't want to kill you guys!

I stuffed a big bite of blueberry muffin in my mouth and concentrated on staring at my carrot sticks. But inside, I was really upset. Didn't my friends know that a person could change?

I guess not, I decided.

Or maybe I was changing—and they weren't.

Right then I had my first pang of homesickness—for White Oak!

No one at White Oak treated me like this, I thought. No one there thought all I could be was a jock.

I tried to talk to Carrie about it at dinner tonight. Dad had a faculty meeting at school.

"Were you ever in any school plays?" I asked her.

"Sure," Carrie said. "All of them. I had big parts, too. Really huge."

"Cool!" I said. "Like what?"

"Well, in the first grade, we did the 'Three Little Pigs'," Carrie said.

"And you were the wolf?" I asked.

"No. I was the house of bricks," she said. "Then in junior high I was a tree in *Into the Woods*. And in high school I was the mountain in some crazy play about climbing Mount Everest. See what I mean? *Big* parts. Gigantic. You get the picture."

I laughed. "So being the mountain was the *peak* of your career?"

"Don't even go there," Carrie said, waving a hand. "Everyone said stuff like that to me."

I jabbed at my plate of macaroni and cheese. "I'm thinking of trying out for *Peter Pan*," I said quietly.

"Great!" Carrie said. "I'd love to see you flying across the stage. Now *that's* what I'd call soaring to new heights!"

"Yeah," I said, nodding. "So how come Amanda, Max, and Brian don't see it that way?"

Carrie popped a forkful of salad into her mouth. "What do you mean?" she asked.

"I told them I was thinking of trying out for the play," I explained. "And they laughed at me!"

"Don't take it too hard," Carrie said. "They were probably just joking around. You've been away for a while, so you've probably forgotten how they can be."

"No, I haven't. They—"

But Carrie kept on talking. "It might take a while to fit back in with your old crowd, after being at White Oak," she said. "Just give it time."

Maybe I don't *want* to fit back in, I thought. Not if it means being shoved into a little box.

Mary-Kate the jock.

That's *part* of me. But not *all* of me.

Boxed-in

Anyway, I let the whole thing drop. Then Carrie started telling me about this Chicago Bulls poster she saw in a shop downtown.

Now she's doing it, too! I thought. She's acting like all I care about is sports!

I wish I could talk to someone else about the school play.

Someone who would understand.

Like Ashley.

But she hasn't called me yet. Not once since I've been home. She hasn't even sent me an E-mail!

So I decided to break down and call *her*. Well, who do you supposed answered the phone at Porter House but Kristin Lindquist, Dana Woletsky's friend. She said she was on a special long-distance call to some guy, but she *promised* to tell Ashley I called.

We'll see.

In the meantime I'm not going to let Amanda, Brian, or Max tell me who I can be. I guess that means I've pretty much decided to try out for the play! I'm a little scared, but excited, too.

The only thing I'm really worried about is: Will I have time to play softball *and* be in the play?

But I can worry about that later—*if* I get a part!

The tryouts are tomorrow, Diary. Wish me luck!

P.S. Wish You Were Here

Dear Diary,

How do I do it? How do I *always* manage to get myself on Ms. Bloomberg's bad side?

Wait till you hear what happened in English class today. We were supposed to turn in our book reports, remember? I could hardly wait. I was so proud of what a great job I'd done.

"Okay, girls," Ms. Bloomberg announced. "Please pass your book reports to the front of the class."

Like I said, I couldn't wait to turn in my paper. I reached into my book bag, and pulled out the folder where I'd put the report.

Then I almost fell off my seat.

My report was *gone*! Missing. As in, not there!

I started to panic. Where is it? I wondered wildly. Did I lose it? Did I leave it somewhere? Did somebody steal it?

Calm down, I told myself. You had it on Monday in the library. It has to be here!

I flipped through my stuff five more times, looking in every single notebook and folder I owned. I even went through all my old math homework. Just in case.

But my book report was gone.

Ms. Bloomberg was staring at me now, waiting for me to turn in my paper.

"Uh, Ms. Bloomberg," I said, raising my hand. "May I be excused? I think I'm going to be sick."

I covered my mouth like I might puke. That always works. No one wants to see *that*!

Ms. Bloomberg nodded quickly, but her lips were pursed kind of tight. I wasn't sure she believed me.

But I couldn't worry about that right now. I had to find my book report and turn it in on time. Or else!

Ms. Bloomberg's rule was, if you didn't hand your paper in when it was due, she lowered your grade. One letter for every day it was late!

As soon as I escaped the classroom, I started running. I tore out of the building and raced across the lawn to Porter House. Luckily, everyone was in class, so the dorm was empty.

I raced up to my room and hunted through everything on my desk. On my shelf. In the drawers.

It wasn't there.

What now? I thought, flopping into my desk chair. A lump formed in my throat.

Then I saw something sticking out of the disk

drive on my computer. The disk with my book report file on it!

Bingo! I thought. I'll just print out another copy!

I ran to the computer lab in Stevens Hall, shivering the whole way. But Mr. Warsowsky was in there, printing out twenty copies of a test for his civics class. I had to hide in the hall until he was done.

Finally, he left and I slipped into the computer lab.

Now, of course, the printer was out of paper.

By the time I loaded more paper and printed my report, I'd been gone from class for thirty minutes. English was almost over!

I raced back to Ms. Bloomberg's class. Outside the room, I stuffed the book report inside my sweater. I mean, I couldn't just walk into class carrying it, could I?

Unfortunately, it was sort of lumpy in there.

And crinkly.

I had to stand up really straight so I wouldn't crush it as I walked.

"Ashley," Ms. Bloomberg said, rather coolly, as I came back into class. "It's nice to have you back. Finally. Are you all right?"

I gulped. Oops, I totally forgot. I was supposed to be sick!

I nodded, trying to look pale. Which was hard, since I'd been racing around outdoors without a jacket. My cheeks were probably bright pink.

Plus, I was out of breath.

I crept to my seat and slid into it. Everyone in the whole class was staring at me.

Were they worried about me? Or just giving me suspicious looks? I couldn't tell.

"So, Ashley, do you have your book report for me?" Ms. Bloomberg asked.

"Um, yes," I said.

But first I had to get it out from under my sweater!

Luckily, I was sitting in the back of the room. Ms. B. couldn't see me very well. So I started a fake coughing fit. At the same time, I "accidentally" dropped my pencil on the floor. Between the coughing and bending over to get my pencil, I managed to yank my book report out from under my sweater.

Unfortunately, it was pretty mangled and wrinkled. But at least I could hand it in on time!

"Thank you, Ashley," Ms. Bloomberg said. She sounded a little sarcastic.

Phoebe shot me a puzzled look from across the

room. She knows me better than anyone at White Oak, now that Mary-Kate is gone. So I guess she knew I'd never have a gross coughing fit all over the place. Not without a good reason, anyway. Or a sneaky one!

Speaking of Mary-Kate, she still hasn't answered my E-mails. I sent her one last night and another one today.

But I got nothing. Just silence.

So I guess it's official. Mary-Kate's not speaking to me.

That hurts. But I'm trying not to think about it. I'm really on my own now.

So what *I* want to know is: What happened to the original copy of my book report?

I've been thinking about it all day. And I can come up with only one explanation.

Jeremy.

I mean, he was the last person who saw it, right? So either he picked it up by accident . . .

Or he took it on purpose. Maybe it was one of his practical jokes.

In which case, Cousin Jeremy is in major trouble.

Chapter 5

Monday

Dear Diary,

You're never going to believe this. I got a part in the play!!

Isn't that fantastic, Diary?

I just found out today. Mr. Ousakian posted the cast list up on the hall bulletin board.

At first, I didn't see my name on the list. That's because I was only looking at the top. But I didn't get the part of Peter. Caitlin Morris did.

Then I saw my name and I got soooooo psyched! I've been practically floating ever since!

Okay, okay. Maybe I should get ahold of myself and tell you the whole story.

The tryouts were Friday after school, in the gym. Mr. Ousakian, the drama teacher, ran the auditions. He is so cool. He makes fun of people, but not in a mean way. He's just really honest.

On Cloud Nine

Like when Jennifer Dilber was reading for the part of Wendy, he called out, "Jennifer! You're *acting* with your hair!"

It was true. She was flinging her hair around like it had the name "Wendy" written all over it!

And when James got up to try out for Captain Hook, Mr. Ousakian grinned at him. "James, you have enough metal attached to you already."

Everyone laughed. James *does* have five earrings. But three of them are fake, not pierced.

Anyway, when it was my turn to read, I thought I'd be really nervous. But I wasn't! I just marched up onto the stage and stood there, with my feet planted apart and my hands on my hips.

That's how Peter Pan always stands. I thought I looked pretty cool.

"Nice, Mary-Kate," Mr. Ousakian said. "But you're going to have a hard time holding your script that way."

"Oh. Right," I said, feeling myself blush. I had to walk over to the table to pick up a script.

"Turn to page thirty-four," Mr. Ousakian said. "I'll read the part of Wendy, and you read Peter's part. From the top."

We did that for a while. Then Mr. Ousakian had me sing "I've Gotta Crow."

The crowing part was hard. My, "er-er-er-errh!" came out kind of squeaky.

That's because Michael Snow was sitting in the auditorium watching! He's this really cute eighth grader. It's funny, but I never noticed him before.

Everyone was really nice to me. I didn't know most of the other kids at the tryouts. There were a lot of eighth graders. And kids who'd been in other plays. You know, the nonjock types.

But after being at White Oak, I'm pretty good at making new friends. So it wasn't a problem.

Ashley's snobby friend Jennifer Dilber hung

Crocodile Crowing

around to watch everyone else try out.

"Nice job, Mary-Kate," she said after my audition. "But your crowing sounded more like a crocodile. Hey, maybe you'll get that part! Wouldn't *that* be cute?"

Ha ha.

Anyway, I wasn't sure I'd get a part at all. That's why I didn't write to you on Friday. I was worried I might jinx things.

But guess what?

I'm going to be Tiger Lily, the Indian princess! The only thing I'm worried about is softball practice. I missed Friday, for the tryouts. And I hate to admit this, but I lied to Amanda about it. I told her I had to make up a math test.

"You're kidding! Mr. Frankel's making you stay

after school on a *Friday* afternoon?" she shrieked.

"Oh, I don't mind," I said quickly. "I want to get it out of the way before the weekend."

Amanda looked at me like I was from Mars.

And, at the game on Saturday, she kept telling me how much they missed me at practice.

"Mary-Kate, you're the glue that holds the team together," she kept saying.

Talk about a guilt trip!

"Don't worry, I'll be there on Monday," I promised her. "And hey, I'm here now!"

It was my turn up at bat. But I struck out. And when I came back to the bench, Amanda gave me a look that said, "If you'd been here for practice, maybe we'd be winning."

We lost the game, four-zip.

When I lied to Amanda on Friday, I told myself that if I didn't get a part in the play, no one would know I'd even tried out.

But now that I *do* have a part, I've been thinking I should come clean with her.

I tried at lunch today.

"Hey, Amanda, remember those tryouts for *Peter Pan*?" I began.

"Oh, I'm so glad you didn't go out for that play,"

Amanda jumped in. "Like I said, you're not the actress type."

"I'm not?" I said, trying not to get mad.

Amanda started on a second piece of pizza. "Nope," she said. "And besides, what if you made a fool of yourself onstage? In front of everyone? That would be the worst, wouldn't it? Definitely stick with sports, Mary-Kate."

Make a fool of myself? I hadn't even thought of that!

Yikes.

Maybe it's better if my friends *don't* know I'm in the play. Not for a while, anyway. Not till I figure out if I can really be an actress!

I did call Ashley again, though. (She never called me back last week—but I decided maybe Kristin never gave her the message.) So I tried again and this time someone put me on hold and then hung up on me!

I've had it, Diary. If Ashley wants to talk to me— she knows where the phone is!

Dear Diary,

I am *so* mad, I can barely write. My hand is shaking too much.

I found out where my book report is!

34

Jeremy took it, just like I thought. He actually *stole* it on purpose! And get this—he turned it in as his own!

I found out the truth this afternoon. I ran into Jeremy just before our history class was starting. We have two classes with the guys from Harrington: history and science lab.

"Hi," I said. "Hey, Jeremy, remember when we were in the library on Wednesday? Did you by any chance accidentally pick up my book report and put it with your stuff?"

His face got red right away. That's when I knew something was wrong.

"Uh, yeah," he mumbled, looking down at his sneakers.

"Jeremy! If this is your idea of a practical joke, I'm going to strangle you!" I said.

"Give me a break!" he snapped at me. "It wasn't a joke. I *needed* it, okay?"

Huh? Then I suddenly realized something. Jeremy was looking totally guilty. Like he'd done something wrong. Really wrong.

"What do you mean, you needed it?" I demanded.

"Shh!" Jeremy said, frowning. "Keep it down, okay?" He glanced around to make sure no one was listening. "Look, I'm sorry, Ashley," he went on. "I was kind of freaked about my book report. It was due today, you know? So I borrowed your paper and turned it in to Mr. March this morning."

I almost passed out from shock. "Jeremy! Are you kidding? It has my name on it!" I cried.

"Not anymore," Jeremy said. "I retyped it and put my name on it. Pretty smart, huh?"

"I don't believe this!" I practically shouted. "Jeremy, that's plagiarism! You know, *stealing* someone else's ideas?"

"Gee, Ash, why don't you take out an ad on MTV?" Jeremy snapped, looking around again.

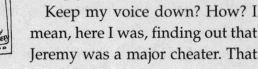 "Keep your voice down, okay?"

Keep my voice down? How? I mean, here I was, finding out that Jeremy was a major cheater. That was bad enough.

But did he have to drag *me* down with him? If Jeremy got caught, I was going to be in deep trouble, too.

My mind raced, trying to figure out what to do.

Turn Jeremy in? Not good. That would be ratting on a relative. Besides, what if Jeremy denied it—and no one believed me? Everyone would think I was in on this stupid scheme!

"You've got to go to your teacher right now," I

said firmly. "And get the book report back."

"No way," Jeremy replied.

"Please," I begged him. "Come on, Jeremy. Before it's too late!"

"Look, just chill, Ashley," Jeremy said. "No one's going to find out about this. We won't get caught. And I'll never do it again, okay?"

Never do it again? But what about this time?

Class was starting, so I couldn't stand there arguing with Jeremy any longer. I had to run.

But after that I was jumpy all day. Every time a teacher even glanced in my direction, I kept thinking, this is it. You're busted, Ashley. Go directly to jail.

Actually, it would probably be worse than that. If I get caught plagiarizing, they'll probably kick me out of White Oak and send me home!

But I can't go back to Chicago. My sister's there—and she's still mad at me!

I'm really upset about this thing with Jeremy, Diary. But I know I'd be okay if I could just talk to Mary-Kate about it.

I was dying to call her today. So I left lunch early and sneaked back to Porter House. With everyone else gone, it was a cinch to get to the phone.

I dialed home and crossed my fingers. But just like last time Mary-Kate wasn't there. I got the answering machine again with that stupid new greeting.

I didn't leave a message. I'm not going to beg Mary-Kate to call me if she won't even answer my E-mails!

But it's driving me crazy that she's never home. Where *is* she after school every day, anyway?

I can't write anymore now, Diary. My stomach is starting to hurt. The Mary-Kate situation is bad enough. But I also can't deal with the fact that Jeremy copied *my* book report!

I know we're both going to get in trouble for this. Unless . . .

Hey, wait! I just got an idea. It's brilliant—an Ashley Burke special!

I'll tell you what happens tomorrow, Diary. Wish me luck!

Chapter 6

Tuesday

Dear Diary,

Still no word from Ashley. She hasn't even *tried* to reach me! Not even by E-mail! The more I think about it, the madder I get.

I'm going to make a new rule: No more writing about Ashley in this diary. From now on she's history!

But something good happened today, Diary.

My first play rehearsal!

It was so cool, sitting there in the dark theater after school, watching the action onstage. Mr. Ousakian had everyone go through the first part of Act I, so they didn't need me yet. (Tiger Lily doesn't come on until Act II.) But even if we're not onstage, Mr. O. wants all cast members to be there.

Of course, that meant I had to miss practice with the Bashers again. I didn't mind, though. It was fun, hanging out with the other actors.

Sara Morgan, a popular eighth grader, sat next to me. Sara's a great dancer and she's an actress in real life, too. She does commercials on TV sometimes. Mr. O. cast her as Tinker Bell.

"Isn't James Wilder gorgeous?" Sara whispered.

 James—the guy with five ear-rings—got the part of Captain Hook. Mr. O. told him he could wear the earrings for the play. He said it would make Hook look like a real pirate.

"James is okay," I said. "Not exactly my type, though."

"He would be if you heard some of the songs he writes," Sara said in a dreamy voice.

It was amazing, Diary. There I was, talking to this superpopular eighth grader, about a supercute boy.

Wouldn't Ashley be jealous? Well she would be if she even cared what was going on in my life!

Whoops. That's the very last time I'm mentioning Ashley. I almost forgot. She's history.

I walked home after rehearsal with a big grin on my face. It was an awesome day—until I ran into Max and Brian. They had just finished softball practice.

I gulped. Had they found out yet about me being in the play?

"Hey, where were you, Mary-Kate?" Max asked.

Phew! They didn't seem to know yet. So far I'd been lucky. The cast list had been posted in the hall at school for two days.

But Max and Brian didn't have a clue. I guess the

two of them are just so into sports, they could care less what anyone else is doing.

So I lied. I don't know why. The words just kind of fell out.

"Mr. Frankel wanted to see me again," I said. "He kept me forever."

Max and Brian nodded sympathetically.

"But you'd better show up tomorrow," Max said. "Coach was asking where you were."

I felt pretty guilty then. But I still want to keep this acting thing to myself—for as long as I can. Which probably won't be long. Amanda will figure it out soon—won't she?

Dear Diary,

Well, there's only one thing I can say after what I did last night.

I must be out of my mind!

And I'm lucky to be here, safe in my dorm room.

Okay, okay. I'd better start at the beginning.

There was only one thing to do about my book report: get it back!

Ideally, I would *rather* have gotten back the one *Jeremy* turned in to Mr. March. But there was no way. The shuttle bus to Harrington doesn't run at night. And I definitely couldn't walk there in the dark.

So I decided to go visit Ms. Bloomberg at home. There was no time to lose, and I couldn't afford to wait until tomorrow.

My plan was simple. Sneak out of the dorm after dinner, creep across campus and find Ms. Bloomberg's house—somehow. (She lives in one of those faculty houses on campus, but I wasn't sure where.) Then convince her to give me my paper back. (I was praying that she hadn't read it yet!) I had a really good excuse, too. I was going to tell her that I had an even better idea for my book report. That I wanted to revise it—and I was sure it would knock her socks off!

(Remind me to strangle Jeremy!)

Then, I was going to beat it back to Porter House before lights-out.

Did I say simple?

See, I *am* out of my mind!

Anyway, I had just slipped into my black jacket when Phoebe showed up.

"Where are you going?" she asked, eyeing me suspiciously.

"I'm going to see Ms. Bloomberg," I said.

"Now?" Phoebe looked at her alarm clock and frowned. It was eight twenty-four, and dark outside. "What for?"

Uh-oh. Good question. I couldn't tell my room-mate the truth. I didn't want *anyone* to know that Jeremy had copied my paper.

So I tried to come up with a good excuse. I glanced around the room. "Uh, Ms. Bloomberg's been out sick," I lied. "So I'm going to take her some brownies."

Luckily, Carrie had just sent me a whole batch of brownies from home. I grabbed the box and tried to get out the door.

But Phoebe blocked it.

"Wait," she said. "You can't go alone. It's too dark out there. I'll come with you."

That's what I like about Phoebe. She really cares about sticking close and being a good friend.

Only *this time* I didn't want her to come along!

But I couldn't think of a good reason to stop her.

Oh, well, I thought. Maybe I can talk to Ms. Bloomberg alone, once we get there.

Getting out of Porter House turned out to be easy. Miss Viola, our housemother, was busy talking to another student, so we practically waltzed out the front door. They don't lock the doors until ten o'clock P.M.

But once we were outside, I started to shiver.

For one thing, the temperature really dropped at night. And there was no moon at all.

"Wow," I said to Phoebe softly. "It's so dark out here. The sky is totally black."

I guess I'm a city girl at heart. In Chicago, it's *never* this dark. The lights from the city always brighten up the sky, no matter what the moon is doing.

Also, I kept hearing twigs snap and branches creak. Spooky.

"Come on, let's hurry," I said, starting to feel a little scared.

Phoebe laughed. "What's wrong, Ashley?" she asked. "It's a beautiful night. You're not freaking out, are you?"

"I just want to take these to Ms. Bloomberg and get back before lights-out," I answered.

Phoebe was enjoying this, I could tell.

"Do you think we're being followed?" she teased, in a ghostly voice.

"Cut it out," I said. I sped up my steps and hurried across the path toward where I thought the faculty cottages were.

But Phoebe wouldn't quit. "Maybe the famous White Oak Breath-Smeller is out," she whispered.

The Breath-Smeller? Huh? Then I remembered.

P.S. Wish You Were Here

The White Oak Breath-Smeller is a legend at school. Mary-Kate and I heard about it not long after we arrived. The Breath-Smeller is supposed to be this hairy creature who lives in the woods. And he can smell chocolate on your breath.

According to the story, he only comes out at night. If you've been eating chocolate, he'll attack.

"Ha ha, Phoebe," I said. "That Breath-Smeller thing is just a joke."

"I don't think so," Phoebe said, shaking her head. "My older sister was here when it attacked Rachel Calloway."

"Really?"

I'd heard about Rachel Calloway. She was part of the legend. As the story goes, she went out late one night, a few years ago. She'd been eating a whole bag of M&M's. And when she came back, she had big scratch marks on her face!

"You mean, it's actually true?" My voice shook a little.

Phoebe nodded. "Definitely," she said.

This whole Breath-Smeller thing probably sounds really dumb, I know. But when you're outside in the dark alone, and you keep hearing strange noises, it isn't so funny!

"At least we haven't been eating choc—" I started to say.

Then I remembered. The brownies! We'd been snacking on them all day!

"And we're carrying them!" Phoebe said really softly.

We passed under a street lamp right then, and I saw a look of terror on Phoebe's face. Maybe she was joking before. But she was scared to death now!

"Where *is* Bloomberg's house, anyway?" Phoebe asked.

We'd been wandering around campus for twenty minutes.

"I'm not sure," I admitted. "I thought it was this way, but . . ."

"We're lost," Phoebe whispered.

"No we're not," I said. "There it is! Number Eleven, Hawthorne Lane!"

We were both so scared, we raced up to Ms. Bloomberg's cottage and pounded on the door.

But the lights were out. And no one was home.

"I thought you said she was sick," Phoebe said, shivering in the dark.

"Uh, she is," I mumbled.

Phoebe glared at me. Her whole face said what

she was thinking: If Bloomberg is sick, why isn't she home in bed?

I didn't know what to say.

"Did you hear that?" Phoebe whispered.

We both turned and listened.

Footsteps. Crunching. Slowly. In the dark. Toward us.

"It's the Breath-Smeller!" Phoebe practically squeaked.

"No way. It's only the security guard." I tried to sound brave.

"Run anyway!" Phoebe answered.

We raced away, scared out of our minds. Back toward Porter House. The whole time, I was praying that we wouldn't be locked out of the dorm all night.

But as we neared the house, I could see that it was already past lights-out.

We tried the front door handle. Locked!

Oh, no! I thought. We're going to get caught!

We stood there for a minute, shivering in the moonlight.

"What now?" Phoebe asked, glaring at me.

SNAP. CRACK!

That's when we heard something moving in the trees just a few feet away.

"The Breath-Smeller!" she whispered.

In a panic we raced up to one of the bedroom windows on the first floor. I knocked softly on the glass.

Someone peered out the window.

It was Brooke Miller, another First Form girl. I'd seen her hanging around, but I barely knew her.

Brooke opened her window. "Hi," she whispered. "What's up?"

"Hi," I said. "We got locked out. Can we come in through your room?"

She shook her head, laughing. I knew what she was thinking: "What a dumb thing to do!"

But we didn't care.

We just wanted to get back in!

Brooke said okay and gave Phoebe a hand. Actually, she was really nice about it.

Then she tried to help me get in.

But it was kind of hard climbing over the bushes and hoisting myself up to the window ledge.

And I was kind of noisy, too. I'd hate to admit that I, Ashley Burke, ever *grunted*. But I did.

Not good. Because just as I was climbing in Angela's window, a light came on in the lounge. I glanced over.

Was that Miss Viola's face watching me?

My stomach did a flip-flop.

Phoebe didn't say a word till we were safely back in our room. Then she put her hands on her hips and glared at me.

"Ms. Bloomberg wasn't even home," she said. "And sick people stay home. What's going on?"

"I-I don't know," I sputtered.

Phoebe waited, tapping her foot.

"Well, it's just that, it's sort of hard to explain," I went on lamely.

Phoebe shrugged. "Okay, fine. Don't tell me," she said. "But next time don't expect me to even think about coming with you."

Then she got into bed and turned out the lights.

I lay there in the dark, feeling really terrible about the whole mess. I can't blame Phoebe for not trusting me now. She knows I lied about why I wanted to go to Ms. Bloomberg's.

She just doesn't know *why*.

How did I get into this disaster?

And how am I going to get out of it?

I wish Mary-Kate were here!

Chapter 7

Friday

Dear Diary,

First of all, I am *not* going to mention That Person. But she still hasn't called me, written me, or even sent me an E-mail! And it's been two weeks!

Now on to my *other* problem.

For the past two days, I've been cutting softball practice to go to play rehearsals.

And I'm feeling really guilty about it.

On Wednesday I told Amanda I had a dentist appointment after school. I even pretended to walk home, then sneaked back to the theater.

Yesterday I ran into Brian and Max after my last class.

"See you at practice," Brian said.

"Oh, gee," I said, trying to fake a sick voice. "I think I'm getting the flu. I might not make it."

Max didn't look very sympathetic. In fact, he actually scowled at me. "Look, Mary-Kate, what did you come home from boarding school for, if you're not going to play ball?" he demanded.

Was he kidding? It seemed like that was the only reason they wanted me back!

I wanted to choke Max, but I couldn't. Not if I

was going to convince him that I was feeling really sick.

"Got to run!" I told him. Then I dashed into the girls' room.

I hid in there until I was sure he was gone. Finally, I went to rehearsal.

But I felt pretty bad about missing all those team practices. So today I did the opposite: I lied to Mr. Ousakian. I told *him* I had a dentist appointment. Then I went to softball practice instead!

It's getting hard to keep all my stories—and all my dentist appointments—straight!

"Well, *finally*," Brian said loudly when I arrived at the field, carrying my glove. "It's about time."

"Welcome back, Mary-Kate!" Coach Latimore said. He sounded really happy to see me.

But that was before I stepped up to bat. I was so rusty, I struck out three times!

By the end of the day, everyone was really mad at me. They said I'd be in a lot better shape if I hadn't missed all those practices.

Strikeout!

And I knew they were right.

We have a game tomorrow. So I've *got* to pull myself together.

But you know what, Diary? I'm not sure that I *can* come through for the Bashers this time.

Not when I'm having so much trouble concentrating on my game!

I even told Carrie to forget about coming to the game tomorrow.

"Why, Mary-Kate?" she asked. "I was looking forward to it."

"Oh, we're playing a totally loser team," I said. "It'll be a complete yawn."

That was another lie to feel guilty about. But the truth is, I don't want Carrie to see me mess up.

What am I going to do, Diary? I can't go on like this . . . but I don't want to quit the play. Acting is more fun than I ever imagined.

I wish I could talk to Coach Latimore about this—that I love the Belmont Bashers, but I'm not just a jock. Don't I have a right to find out what other talents I might have?

But Coach has always made his position clear. The team has to come first.

I'm too grumpy to write any more tonight. But it's not your fault, Diary. It's you-know-who's fault.

Why hasn't she even called me once? Doesn't she know that I need her advice sometimes? Like right now.

But hey, I'm so mad at her for not calling, I don't think I'd even speak to her if she *did*!

Dear Diary,

I'm in *big* trouble.

I got a note from Ms. Bloomberg today. She didn't say a word—she just handed it to me as I walked out of her English class.

The note said: "Ashley—Please see me at 4:00 tomorrow afternoon. We have something important to discuss."

Stomach Flip-Flop Number ???!

I kept rereading the note, looking for clues. I bet she had read the paper by now. Had she found out about Jeremy stealing my book report? I couldn't tell.

What if she thinks *I'm* the one who plagiarized?

I guess I'll find out tomorrow. Going to see a teacher on a *Saturday*—that's pretty bad!

And by the way, I've given up on Mary-Kate. I sent her two more E-mails, but she didn't answer them.

If she wants to be that way, fine. I'll never speak to her again.

Chapter 8

Saturday

Dear Diary,

It's after lights-out and I'm in bed, writing by flashlight. Phoebe is awake, I can tell. But I can't talk to her about what's keeping me awake. I can't talk to anyone.

I was supposed to go see Ms. Bloomberg at four o'clock, remember? I was so nervous all day. Waiting.

I had so many butterflies in my stomach that I  couldn't eat a thing at lunch. Which is too bad, because the food today was amazing.

That's because there were a whole bunch of parents visiting White Oak. They came to see if they wanted to send their kids here next year.

We had blueberry pancakes for breakfast, and hot roast beef, gourmet pizza, and ice-cream sundaes for lunch.

Like I said, I couldn't eat a bite. Can you believe it?

Phoebe was no help, either. She's been reading this story by Edgar Allen Poe, called "The Tell-Tale Heart." It's all about this guy who kills someone and buries him under the floor of his house. And then the murderer feels so guilty, he keeps hearing a heart beating really loud. He thinks it's the dead person's heart!

Thump! Thump!

Creepy, huh?

Anyway, ever since that night we went to Ms. Bloomberg's house, Phoebe's been watching me like a hawk. She says when people are guilty, it shows all over their faces.

"So Ashley, why aren't you eating?" she asked me. "Feeling guilty about something?"

She was just kidding, I think.

"It's my new diet," I lied. "I can only eat canned food. This stuff is fresh, so it's off my list. Bummer."

Phoebe just shrugged. But she looked kind of hurt. She knows I've been keeping a major secret from her.

But what can I do? I can't tell my roommate about Jeremy copying my paper. I mean, she hates him already. What if she ratted on him?

Besides, I don't think Phoebe would understand. She'd probably tell me to turn him in myself or something.

Forget Phoebe right now, I told myself. You've got a much bigger problem: Ms. Bloomberg.

By the time four o'clock rolled around, I was so nervous, my heart was beating really hard. Just like in that spooky story.

But when I got to Ms. Bloomberg's office, she wasn't there. The door was locked, and there was a note taped to it.

It said: "Ashley—Sorry, but I have an emergency. We'll have to postpone our meeting until Monday."

Monday? That's two whole days away! How am I supposed to wait that long?

I'll probably have a heart attack by then!

Dear Diary,

Wildwood Ravens, 3—Belmont Bashers, 2.

That was the score when we lost our game today. And it was totally my fault.

I am *so* mortified.

I came up to bat in the bottom of the ninth, with two people on base. The Ravens were ahead by one run. It was up to me to slug the ball into oblivion so we'd win the game.

I hit a tiny pop fly instead. Right into the pitcher's glove!

(I can't believe I'm actually writing all this down! It was so humiliating. All I wanted to do was sink into the ground and disappear.)

To make things worse, nobody on the team spoke to me after the game. I guess I'd really let them down by missing so many practices. But they didn't have to be so mean about it.

So what am I supposed to do?

I *can't* give up softball. The Bashers are counting on me.

And I can't give up the play, either! It wouldn't be fair to the other cast members. I don't want to let them down.

Besides, I'm determined to show everyone I'm not just a jock. I can do other stuff, too.

My Tiger Lily costume is awesome! Just wait till . . .

Whoops. I almost forget my new rule. I was about to mention *her*. Let's just call her "A." I was going to say, wait till *A.* sees my costume. She'll be so jealous.

But obviously she couldn't care less about me. And she'll never see my costume anyway. She's 800 miles away.

Help, Diary! You're my only friend now. What should I do?

Diary? Hello?

Chapter 9

Monday

Dear Diary,

Remember I said I never wanted to speak to Mary-Kate again?

Well, I changed my mind. I'll speak to her. But she has to call me first!

I just got off my computer. I sent Mary-Kate a really long, detailed E-mail. I told her everything that's happened to me lately. All about Jeremy stealing my paper.

And my nightmare meeting today with Ms. Bloomberg!

I was so nervous when I walked into her office.

"Hi, Ms. Bloomberg," I said. My voice almost squeaked.

"Oh, hello, Ashley," she said. "I'm glad you're here. Please sit down. I have something very nice to tell you."

Nice?

I sat down. And held my breath.

"I just wanted to let you know that I loved your book report on *The Old Man and the Sea*. It was a wonderful piece of writing. So I've decided to submit your paper for the annual White Oak/Harrington English prize."

Ms. Bloomberg likes me! She really likes me! "Awesome!" I started to say.

But then it hit me.

"Did you say, um, the White Oak/*Harrington* prize?" I practically choked the words out.

"Yes." Ms. Bloomberg nodded. "The English teachers from both schools submit their best students' work. Then we all read the submissions. After that, we get together to vote on the best one."

My heart started pounding superfast. Just like in that Edgar Allen Poe story.

"What's wrong, Ashley?" Ms. Bloomberg asked me.

I gulped. "Oh, nothing," I said. "Nothing at all. Is that why you wanted to see me?"

"Well, yes." The corners of my teacher's mouth curved up, just slightly. I guess, for Ms. Bloomberg, that was a smile. "Unless you need to talk to me about something else?" she added.

"Yes. I mean, no. And thank you for warning me—I mean, telling me," I blurted.

Ms. Bloomberg looked at me a little strangely. But then she nodded. "Good luck, Ashley," she said.

I think I'm up to stomach flip-flop number twenty-nine by now.

As soon as Mr. March reads my book report, he'll know that Jeremy and I turned in the same paper, I thought.

I just couldn't let that happen.

So later in the afternoon, when we went over to Harrington for class, I decided to take matters into my own hands.

Normally, I get really psyched when we go to Harrington, because it's my chance to scope out the guys. But today I scanned the walkways hoping to spot Jeremy.

Finally I saw him.

"Jeremy!" I hurried over to him. "We are in such trouble," I said.

"No kidding," he answered glumly. "I've got bad news. Mr. March loved my book report—I mean, *your* book report—so much, he's submitting it for the White Oak/Harrington English prize."

Flip-flop number thirty.

"Are you serious?" I practically shouted. "I *told* you we'd get into huge trouble! Ms. Bloomberg is submitting mine, too!"

"Oh, man," Jeremy said, pounding his head. "I'm sorry, Ashley. I didn't think it would turn out this way."

My cousin *did* seem sorry. But I didn't care.

"There's only one thing to do," I told him.

"What?"

"Do I have to spell it out for you?" I asked. "You've got to confess! Go to Mr. March and tell him the truth!"

Jeremy shook his head. "No way," he said. "We just stay mum. If we both say we wrote the paper, they'll never be able to prove who copied it."

My cousin can be a real jerk.

"Jeremy!" I yelled. "That's nuts!"

"Shh!" he said, glancing around quickly. A teacher was hurrying across the quad, on his way to class.

"Look," I said, lowering my voice. "Even if they don't know who really wrote it—which was *me*, by the way—they'll still know that *someone* copied. So, we'll both be accused of cheating."

Jeremy shook his head and started to walk away. "I say we chill," Jeremy said, over his shoulder. "Maybe they'll never catch us. Gotta go. Bye!"

Right then I didn't care that Jeremy was my cousin. I was so mad, I was ready to strangle him! The only thing that stopped me was the tiny hope that Mary-Kate could come up with a better idea.

One that didn't involve a funeral!

Mary-Kate's so smart about stuff like this. And she's the only one who'd understand how to deal with Jeremy.

I'm going to check my E-mail again right now. Maybe she's answered me already. I mean, after I poured my guts out to her like that, she'll have to talk to me. Won't she?

Chapter 10

Tuesday

Dear Diary,

I'm a nervous wreck—and it's all Mary-Kate's fault. If she'd just call me, maybe we could think of some way out of this mess.

But instead, I just walk around all day, waiting for the ax to fall. I know as soon as Ms. Bloomberg reads Jeremy's book report—or Mr. March reads mine— it's all over for me.

I am so freaked out, I'm ready to grovel to Mary-Kate again. I'm going to send her fifty E-mails tonight. And they'll all say the same thing.

"Mary-Kate, call me! PLEASE! I need your help!"

Dear Diary,

Okay, here's what I wish.

I wish I'd never left White Oak.

I wish I hadn't lied to everybody: my friends, my coach, and my drama teacher.

I wish someone understood how hard it is to make the right decisions all the time. And I wish you-know-who would write or call me soon!

This is incredible, Diary.

I haven't heard one word from A. for two-and-a-half weeks. How can she just dump me like this?

I don't get it.

Things are so messed up right now, I'd do anything to talk with her.

Today Coach Latimore and Mr. Ousakian both found out the truth.

First, Mr. Ousakian called me out into the hall during my sixth-period French class.

"Mary-Kate," he said, in a really serious tone of voice. "We've got a problem."

"We do?" I asked. I tried to look innocent, but I guess it didn't work.

"Yes," Mr. Ousakian said. "And we need to solve it very soon. It's about rehearsals."

"Oh. I, um, well, I've got this . . ." I stammered.

"Hold it," Mr. Ousakian stopped me, putting up a hand. "Let me save you the trouble of making up another lie about why you won't be at rehearsal this afternoon. You're on a softball team of some sort, and you have a game."

I hope I look good in red, Diary. Because I knew that's what color my face was!

I was so surprised, I didn't know what to say. So I just blurted, "How did you find out?"

"We won't get into that," Mr. Ousakian answered. "Let's just say, a cast member knows someone on your softball team."

At first I thought, Who's the rat? But then I figured, hey, whoever it is is just looking out for the play.

"Mary-Kate, I thought I made it clear to everyone in the beginning," Mr. Ousakian went on. "If you want to be in the play, you have to attend *all* the rehearsals. I'm afraid you're going to have to choose. Softball or *Peter Pan*. You can't do both."

"But—" I tried to think of a good argument. I couldn't, though.

I mean, for one thing, I knew I'd be letting the whole cast down this afternoon. Big time. Tiger Lily had a big scene in the act they were supposed to rehearse this afternoon. And I wasn't going to be there.

Mr. Ousakian gave me his famous squinty-eyed stare, and crossed his arms over his chest.

"I'll give you until Friday to decide," he said. Then he nodded at me and left.

Here's another wish, Diary. I wish that was all the news I have to report. But it's not.

When I got to the softball game, Coach Latimore called me aside. And he said the exact same thing as

Mr. Ousakian! Somehow, he'd found out about the play.

"Choose, Mary-Kate," Coach said. "Softball or this drama thing. You can't do both."

It sounded like he was waiting for an answer on the spot!

"Uh, can I have a couple of days to make up my mind?" I asked. "Mr. Ousakian is giving me till Friday."

Coach rolled his eyes. But finally he nodded. The game was about to start.

Softball or Peter Pan?

The good thing about Coach Latimore is that he doesn't hold grudges. He says what he has to say. Then he lets the whole thing go.

So, he treated me just like normal during the game.

Luckily, I got three big hits. The Bashers won, five to two. Yay!!!

But as we were leaving the field, Coach came up to me. "I really hope you'll choose softball, Mary-Kate," he said. "You've just got so much talent as an athlete."

"Thanks, Coach," I said.

I know he was trying to compliment me. But all

he did was make me feel guilty.

Ouch. I'm getting writer's cramp from putting all this down! I guess I'd better get some ZZZs.

But how am I supposed to sleep? I keep worrying about my big decision.

How can I ever choose between softball and the play?

That's my last wish, Diary.

I wish I didn't have to choose.

Chapter 11

Wednesday

Dear Diary,

Help!!! I'm getting deeper and deeper in trouble every day!

Today I got called into the head-mistress's office.

"Do you know why you're here, Ashley?" Mrs. Prichard said in that stern voice she uses when she's lecturing.

"I think so," I admitted. My voice actually cracked, I was trembling so much.

I almost blurted *everything* out. I wanted to say, "It's not my fault, Mrs. Prichard, honest! I didn't give my book report to Jeremy. He stole it and retyped it himself. I would never, ever cheat like that. *Please* don't send me home. It's all my cousin's fault!"

But my throat closed up from nervousness. So I didn't say anything.

"Well, you know the rules here at White Oak, Ashley," Mrs. Prichard said. "Students are not allowed out of their dorms after lights-out. Under any circumstances."

My mouth dropped open in surprise. It wasn't about the book report! It was just about sneaking back into Porter House after hours!

That wasn't so bad. Right?

"Uh, I can explain that, Mrs. Prichard," I said.

Her eyebrows shot up. "Oh, really?" she said. "How?"

"See, I'm, um, thinking of doing a science project about the moon next term," I said  quickly. "So I went outside to see what phase the moon was in. But, um . . . there were so many clouds that I couldn't see it. . . . So I had to wait . . . and I, um, lost track of time."

Mrs. Prichard's expression hadn't changed. I had no idea what she was thinking. Did she believe me?

But I had to keep going. I was on a roll now.

"You know what, Mrs. Prichard?" I rushed on. "I got *so* caught up in staring at the moon, that I *never* wanted to come back inside."

The headmistress raised her eyebrows again. "I see," was all she said.

"So I'm thinking of becoming an astronomer  someday," I babbled. "I mean, I can actually picture it. Me, alone with some giant telescope on a mountain somewhere, watching the stars all night. What a life!"

Mrs. Prichard just sighed. I don't think she believed me one bit. And she looked really tired. "Don't let it happen again, Ashley," she said.

"Oh, I won't," I promised.

I waited for Mrs. Prichard to move on to the next subject. My book report.

But the headmistress picked up a notepad on her desk and wrote me a late pass.

"Give this to your teacher, Ashley," she said. She handed me the slip of paper.

I practically flew back to class.

But you know what, Diary? I didn't feel happy or relieved at all. I felt sick.

I kept watching over my shoulder for the rest of the day. I was just waiting for Ms. Bloomberg or Mrs. Prichard to come up and say, "Ashley Burke, we need to talk to you. *Now!*"

It's only a matter of time before they realize that something fishy has gone on. And Jeremy and I will be in humongous trouble.

Diary, I am so scared I'm going to be expelled from White Oak.

It almost makes me want to cry. Whoops! That is a tear that just fell on this page. It smeared the ink. Sorry.

I can't think of anything worse than being

expelled. I don't want to leave White Oak—I *love* it here!

And I *really* don't want to go back home to live with Mary-Kate. She didn't answer a single one of my pleas for help. Obviously, she hates my guts. *Still*.

Dear Diary,

Guess what?

Ashley doesn't hate me after all!

At least, I don't *think* she does.

I just logged on to check my E-mail and there were about fifty messages from her! They all said, "Call me!"

She sent them a long time ago, though. I guess something was wrong with my E-mail. A couple of days ago I got a message saying the server was down. Whatever that means. Anyway I just got all of Ashley's messages today.

I tried to call Ashley the minute I read those E-mails. Especially after I read the one about some trouble she's in because of Jeremy.

I dialed the main number at White Oak. It was after nine-thirty at night.

Mrs. Prichard answered. Uh-oh.

"Hello, Mrs. Prichard?" I said, really politely. "This is Mary-Kate Burke. May I please speak to Ashley?"

You know how you can just tell when a grown-up is going to say no?

Well, that's the way it was with Mrs. Prichard.

"Is it a family emergency?" she asked. "Because it's almost lights-out, Mary-Kate."

I guess I wasn't thinking very fast. So I told the truth and said no.

Mrs. Prichard clicked her tongue. "You should know better than to call this number just to chat with your sister," she said. "You do remember the rules here at White Oak, don't you, Mary-Kate? Even if you did decide to leave us."

"B-but—" I stammered.

"I'm sorry, Mary-Kate. Perhaps you can write your sister a letter. I'm sure she'd love to hear from you," Mrs. Prichard said. "Good night."

Then she hung up.

Bummer! I felt so dumb. I really blew that one.

I sent Ashley a quick E-mail, but I'm pretty sure she won't get it tonight. She's probably already in bed.

I've got to think of some way to reach Ashley tomorrow.

I'm sure there's a family emergency coming up. I just can't figure out what it will be!

Chapter 12

Thursday

Dear Diary,

Mary-Kate finally did it!

She called me tonight!

My stomach was on about flip-flop number two hundred when Miss Viola knocked on my door. It was right after dinner.

"Ashley, there's a telephone call for you," she said. Her face was all serious. "Your baby-sitter, Carrie, is on the phone."

I followed Miss Viola to her room downstairs. She waited outside in the hall, so I could talk to Carrie in privacy.

Oh no! I thought. Something terrible must have happened! Is Dad okay? Maybe it's Mary-Kate!

I picked up the phone, my heart pounding.

"Hello?" I said.

"Hi, Ashley," Carrie said cheerfully. "Hold on. Here's Mary-Kate."

Mary-Kate? I froze—until I heard my sister's voice.

"Hello?" I said carefully.

"Ashley?" Mary-Kate blurted out. "I'm so sorry I didn't call you sooner! My E-mail was messed up. I didn't get *any* of your messages until last night!"

Ohhhh! That made total sense. So Mary-Kate hadn't blown me off, after all. I was instantly happy!

"I thought you hated me!" I said.

"I thought *you* hated *me*," Mary-Kate answered.

We both laughed. What a relief! Being mad at each other was so horrible.

Then I thought of something. "How come you didn't get the message I left on the answering machine?" I asked.

I heard Mary-Kate talking to Carrie in the background. Sort of arguing, actually. I guess Carrie forgot to tell Mary-Kate that I called.

But I didn't care. I was so glad that Mary-Kate and I were friends again! It was the best.

But I knew Miss Viola wouldn't stay in the hall forever. So I got right to the point.

"Mary-Kate, what am I going to do about this book report mess?" I moaned. "Jeremy and I haven't gotten caught yet. But I just know we will."

"He has to confess," Mary-Kate said. "That's the only way."

"He won't do it," I told her. "I've tried and tried to convince him."

"Well, then, let *me* try," Mary-Kate said.

She put me on hold for a minute while she

74

turned the call into a three-way. In no time at all, Jeremy was on the other line.

I *love* the phone company. There are so many great things you can do with your phone, if you know how. And Mary-Kate sure does!

Now all three of us could talk at once.

"Jeremy, you worm," Mary-Kate said. "You'd better come clean about stealing Ashley's book report. Or else."

"Or else what?" he wanted to know.

"Or else Ashley and I will suddenly remember all the dorky things you've done in your life. Like that time last year, when you thought you were putting on men's cologne for the sixth-grade dance. But you put on your mom's perfume instead!"

I giggled. "Yeah, and you put on way too much of it, too," I added. "You really stunk up the place."

"So what?" Jeremy said. "No one knows about that here at Harrington."

"Not *yet*," Mary-Kate warned him. "Because Ashley is still on the school newspaper staff, remember? And if you don't do the right thing, she'll write an article about you that no one will ever forget!"

Wow, I thought. Great threat, Mary-Kate! Of course, I'd never actually *do* that. I'd never publish dirt on a relative.

Whoa! What am I saying? That's *exactly* what I did last month! I wrote all about Mary-Kate's secret crush in my stupid gossip column!

Jeremy must have remembered that, too. He was quiet for about thirty seconds. I guess he thought I was capable of just about anything!

"Okay," he said finally. "I'll think about it."

"Don't just think about it. *Do* it," Mary-Kate told him. "Now hang up, worm. I need to talk to Ashley alone."

As soon as Jeremy was gone, I burst out laughing.

"We really do have some good stuff on him!" I told Mary-Kate.

"Hey, that was just the tip of the iceberg!" she said.

"But I'd never really write stuff like that about someone. Never again, I mean," I corrected. "I learned my lesson. I'm really sorry about what happened last month."

"Forget it," Mary-Kate said. She sounded like she had finally forgiven me now. For real. "Hey, remember when Jeremy put all those whoopie cushions around the house at Thanksgiving? But *he* was the one . . ."

Mary-Kate didn't have to finish her sentence. I knew what she was talking about. I immediately started cracking up.

"Anyway," Mary-Kate went on. "I've got to talk to you about something else. Something really important."

But before she could tell me, Miss Viola came in. And Mrs. Prichard was right behind her!

Miss Viola looked worried. But Mrs. Prichard was glaring at me.

Uh-oh, I thought. Big trouble!

"Ashley, what's going on here?" Mrs. Prichard asked.

"Oh, nothing," I said, covering up the receiver. I tried hard to keep a straight face. But I was still giggling about Jeremy.

"I heard uproarious laughter from all the way out in the hall!" Mrs. Prichard went on. "I hardly think this sounds like a family emergency. May I please speak to Carrie again?"

"Uh, Carrie?" I said into the receiver. Suddenly, I was feeling a little nervous.

"I thought so," Mrs. Prichard said. "You aren't

really talking to Carrie, are you? Time to hang up."

"But—" I tried to argue.

It was useless. Mrs. Prichard held her hand out for the phone. And she's not the kind of person you say no to.

I handed the receiver to her.

But right before she took it, I heard Mary-Kate shout, "Check your E-mail tonight!"

That reminds me, Diary. I'd better go. I've got to get on-line and find out what the story is with Mary-Kate. It sounds like she has some kind of major problem, too. Hope I can help!

Dear Diary,

I am soooo tired! Today was good and bad. Mostly good though.

First I had a math test that I wasn't exactly ready for. That was the bad part.

But the good part of the day was when I finally talked to Ashley!

What can I say? My sister's the best! She wasn't even mad at me all that time. It was just a dumb E-mail problem.

Anyway, Diary, I'm way too exhausted to tell you all the details of our phone call. I think I definitely helped her with the Jeremy thing. He's being a real jerk, though. So I'm not sure he'll turn himself in.

But after we got on-line tonight, Ashley and I worked everything out. We stayed up half the night, typing back and forth to each other.

I told Ashley everything—about the ultimatums from Coach Latimore and Mr. O. And how I was supposed to choose between my two favorite things. Softball and the play. By tomorrow!

"No way," Ashley typed. "You should do both."

Then she came up with an idea of how to do it.

"You've got to make Coach an offer he can't refuse," she typed.

Like I said, I'm too tired to tell you everything now. But I sure hope Ashley's plan works!

I'll write again tomorrow. Wish me luck!

Chapter 13

Friday

Dear Diary,

Phew! Thanks to Mary-Kate, I'm not going to be expelled from White Oak. Thank you, thank you, thank you, Mary-Kate!

How can I ever repay her?

To make a long story short, Jeremy finally fessed up today.

He wasn't going to, the rat! But I was one step ahead of him. I'd already made a list of embarrassing things to put in the *Acorn*. I flashed it in his face, and he finally came to his senses.

It was lucky that Jeremy came clean now, too. Before Mr. March or Ms. Bloomberg figured it out for themselves. They told him that coming forward on his own, before he was caught, made a big difference.

"But I'm still getting an F on my book report," Jeremy complained to me.

I was stunned. Did he really think I'd feel *sorry* for him? After all he'd put me through? "Like that's my fault?" I said.

Jeremy shrugged. "I guess I *should* have read my

own book," he admitted. "And written my own report."

I didn't even bother answering him. I mean, what was the point? Our cousin is totally clueless.

Jeremy's also under house arrest (the Harrington version of "grounded") for the rest of the month. No parties, no dances, no soccer games. But at least he didn't get expelled.

The two of us were standing outside in the middle of the Harrington campus. I was there to meet Ross and some of his friends for a movie.

"You've got to do one more thing," I told Jeremy.

"What?"

"Explain the whole thing to Phoebe," I said. "So she won't think I'm a criminal."

Jeremy rolled his eyes. He likes Phoebe about as much as she likes him. As in, not at all. But Phoebe was walking toward us, and he couldn't get out of it. So he caved.

Yay! Now Phoebe doesn't hate me anymore, either!

Mary-Kate is a genius. Her plan worked perfectly.

But, did *my* plan work out for her?

Two of a Kind Diaries

Dear Diary,

What a day.

From the minute I got to school this morning, Max, Brian, and Amanda were on my case.

"Are you coming to practice?" Max demanded.

"I'll be there," I said, trying to sound cheery. "You can always count on me."

"Since when?" Amanda shot back.

"Look, I *said* I'm coming to practice! What more do you want from me?" I said.

"How about your autographed program from last year's World Series," Max asked.

Ha! Very funny.

"So you've quit the play!" Amanda announced. She gave me a big smile. "Great!"

"I never said that!" I answered quickly. "I'm still trying to work things out."

Amanda shook her head. "Come on, Mary-Kate. What's it going to be? The team or that dumb play?"

Both, I wanted to say.

But just then the bell rang. We all had to hurry to class. *Saved!* I told myself with a sigh of relief.

Right after school, I went to see Mr. Ousakian.

"I want to stay in the play," I told him. "But I need to take one more afternoon off. Just so I can talk to Coach Latimore."

"Okay, Tiger Lily," Mr. Ousakian said. "But this is the last time. After today, if you don't show up, I'm giving Caroline Mobley the part."

"I'll be here," I promised. Then I raced out of school.

I ran practically all the way to the softball field. I needed to get there early, so I could talk to Coach Latimore alone.

"Well, Mary-Kate," he said, as I arrived, breathless. "I'm glad to see you. Does this mean you've decided to stick with the Belmont Bashers?"

"I hope so," I said, sort of nervously.

"Hope so? I don't like the sound of that," Coach said, frowning.

I thought really hard, trying to remember what Ashley had told me to say. Then I took a deep breath.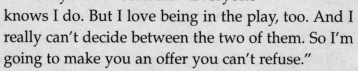

"Here's the thing, Coach," I said. "I really love softball. Everyone knows I do. But I love being in the play, too. And I really can't decide between the two of them. So I'm going to make you an offer you can't refuse."

Coach shot me a sideways glance. Then he went

on with what he'd been doing. Laying out the bats and balls.

"I'm listening," he said.

"I'm willing to get my batting back into shape by practicing with the Belmont Bullets—the under fourteens team," I explained. "They practice at five-thirty every day, right?"

"Right," Coach said slowly.

"That way, I'll be able to go to play rehearsal at three-thirty. And then come here to get my other skills in shape. Working out with older players will make my batting better. They have better pitchers," I added.

Then I took another deep breath, and threw in the clincher. The hard-sell line Ashley had told me to try.

"I want to do everything I can to help out the team," I said. "But I'm not going to give up *Peter Pan*, no matter what. Take it or leave it."

Take it or leave it?

I can't believe I actually had the nerve to say that!

But it worked! Coach stared at me for a long time. Then he let out a sigh. "Okay," he said. "On one condition. You can't miss a single one of the under fourteens team practices."

"No problem!" I told him happily. Then I reached

up and slapped him five.

Coach chuckled and walked away. "You drive a hard bargain, Burke," he said. "But I guess you're worth it."

So that's it! Ashley's plan worked! I can play ball *and* be in the play! Isn't that the best?

Now all I have to worry about is what my friends are going to say when they see me as Tiger Lily.

They'll probably tease me no matter how good I am!

Chapter 14

Thursday
Three weeks later

Dear Diary,

Don't even *ask* why I haven't written for three weeks! It's been so crazy here. Rehearsals, homework, practices— Phew!

But I've been having a great time anyway.

Now I've got to get to work on a book report for English class. Too bad I can't use Ashley's. Just kidding! But I had to tell you that the Bashers won our last three games. And that means we're headed toward the championships! Cool, huh? And everyone says it's thanks to me. I scored a home run in the last game.

I guess my hitting is baaa-aaack!

Now all I have to worry about is

Home run! Peter Pan. What if I'm the worst Tiger Lily ever onstage? My friends will never let me hear the end of it.

Yikes!

Chapter 15

Friday
One week later

Dear Diary,

You'll never believe where I am right now. Back home and writing to you from my own bed!

And Mary-Kate is right across the room in *her* bed, writing in *her* diary!

Just like old times.

It feels so good to be home.

Gosh, I have so much to tell you! I haven't been able to write for the past few weeks, because I had so much work at White Oak. I was crazed, studying for finals. But I got through them.

And I won the White Oak/Harrington English prize!

I was so lucky. Ms. Bloomberg didn't hold it against me that Jeremy had copied my paper! She said she knew I'd never do anything like that. And my book report was the best of all the entries.

Could it be possible I'm actually on good terms with Ms. Bloomberg now?

Anyway, the semester at White Oak is over. I flew home today—just in time to see the opening night of *Peter Pan*!

The play was great. And Mary-Kate was awesome! (I wonder if she'd let me have her Tiger Lily costume. Carrie told me it has 684 beads on it!)

It was great visiting my old school again and seeing my Chicago friends. The whole seventh grade showed up for opening night, and we all sat together.

But the best part was seeing the look of total shock on Mary-Kate's face when I went backstage after the play. She had no idea I was coming. And I guess she was blown away!

"Ashley!" she screamed, when she saw me. "What are *you* doing here?"

"You were fabulous!" I said. I ran up and gave her a huge hug. Then I handed her a huge bouquet of flowers.

"This is the *best*!" Mary-Kate said. "Now you can come to the cast party with me!"

So that's what I did. Dad even let the two of us stay out till midnight. (There were tons of parents there to supervise the party and drive everyone home.) The party was held in a pizza place, and they let us take over a whole room.

And I got to eat Chicago pizza again! It's the best.

So I am totally happy. Well, *almost* totally happy.

There's one sad thing. Being back home makes me realize how much I've missed Mary-Kate. I can't imagine going back to White Oak in the fall without her.

I wish she'd decide to come back with me. But that will never happen. She's having too much fun here. . . .

Dear Diary,

Tonight was one of the best nights of my life.

The play was a big hit!

I *loved* being onstage, Diary. Everything was so cool. Acting, saying my lines, wearing makeup, waiting in the wings with the rest of the cast. It was a major thrill.

All my friends—even my buddies from the Bashers—were in the audience. Amanda sat in the front row, smiling at me the whole time. Even Max and Brian were there!

And nobody laughed at me. When

we took our bows at the final curtain, I heard my friends cheering and whistling extra loud for me. And they all rushed up to me backstage.

"Congratulations, Mary-Kate!" Amanda said. "You were awesome!"

"Thanks," I said.

"No, really," Amanda said. "Listen, Mary-Kate, I'm sorry I said those things. You know, about you just being a jock. I think I was . . . well . . ."

"What?" I asked.

"Jealous," Amanda admitted. "To tell you the truth, I've always wanted to be in the school plays. But I never had the guts to try out."

"Hey," I said. "Forget it. I'm really glad you came."

I squeezed her hand, and Amanda gave me another smile. We were friends again.

The best part, though, came a few seconds later—when I got the shock of my life.

Ashley was there! She and Dad and Carrie had planned the whole thing.

My mouth fell open. I almost started to cry, I was so happy.

Having my sister there to see me as Tiger Lily made the whole night totally perfect.

And you know what else? This may sound

weird, but it was so good to see Ashley's *face*—even though I see almost the same one in the mirror every day!

I'd missed my sister so much.

Of course, I invited Ashley to the cast party. Technically, only cast members and stage crew are invited. But I knew everyone would understand.

Anyway, all through the party, I couldn't stop thinking about everything that's happened to us lately. And how much I'd missed Ashley. Life just isn't as much fun without her.

And I realized something else, too. As much as I like my friends here, the Bashers, and my old school, I still miss White Oak!

There are so many new things I can experience there. I bet I can join a theater group there, too! And I'm ready to do some exploring.

So I've made a decision, Diary. I'm going back to White Oak in the fall.

I can't wait to tell Ashley about this. In fact, I'm going to tell her right now!

P. S. Later—I just told Ashley about my big decision. She almost fell through the floor, she was so surprised. But she was really happy, too.

And so am I.

Now let's just hope that White Oak will take both of us back!

I'll keep you posted, Diary.

Later!

Totally
Cool!

#12 *The Cool Club*

"Did you bring a flashlight?" Ashley whispered in the hallway that night.

"Nope," Mary-Kate whispered back. "Why?"

"It's dark outside," Ashley replied. "We need it to find Elise and her friends behind the Computer Center."

"Ashley, get real," Mary-Kate said. "They're the Glitter Girls! How can we miss them?"

The twins slipped out the side door. Once outside, Mary-Kate yanked the hood of her sweatshirt over her head. It was late September and the New England nights were getting cool.

"All systems go!" she told Ashley.

The fall leaves made crunching sounds as the girls scurried away from Porter House toward the Computer Center.

"Where are they?" Mary-Kate asked Ashley when they reached the big glass-and-brick building. "They said—"

"Greetings, pledges!" Elise Van Hook's voice interrupted.

Mary-Kate whirled around. The four Glitter Girls were stepping out from behind the building and out of the shadows. Elise was wearing a denim jacket with a colorful glitter design. Her eyelids were coated with purple-glitter shadow and her lips sparkled with a glittery pink gloss.

Forget the flashlights, Mary-Kate thought. *I should have worn shades!*

"The time has come," Elise Van Hook said solemnly. "Now let's all join hands and recite the Glitter Girls oath!"

Mary-Kate felt a bit silly when they joined hands. She hadn't taken an oath since she'd gotten her first library card!

"We have gathered tonight as the secret society of Glitter Girls!" Elise announced. "Shine, shine, glimmer, glimmer! Power glows where we shimmer!"

Are they serious? Mary-Kate wondered.

After the oath, Elise explained the rules: "Rule number one: Never, ever talk about Glitter Girls!

95

Rule number two: Wear glitter every day!"

Ashley held up her hands. She was wearing pink glitter nail polish. "Ta-daaa!" she said. "I'm way ahead of you!"

"Nice start, Ashley," Elise said. She reached into her pocket and pulled out a small clear plastic bag filled with Bodacious Blue glitter. "But that's just the beginning!"

Mary-Kate watched as Elise reached into the bag and pinched a clump of glitter between her fingers.

"Prepare to be anointed!" Elise declared. She reached out and sprinkled the blue glitter over Mary-Kate's and Ashley's heads. "Arise, Glitter Girls!"

"Hey!" Mary-Kate said. She coughed as some glitter flew up her nostrils. "Easy with that stuff!"

But Ashley seemed to love it! "Look at me! I'm a Glitter Girl!" she squealed.

"Not so fast!" Elise said. "You can't become members until you go through a whole week of special challenges."

"Excuse me?" Mary-Kate said. "You never said anything about special challenges."

Elise nodded at two of the other girls. They slipped behind the building and returned holding two jars—one with peanut butter, one with dill pickles!

Mary-Kate's heart sank. She couldn't imagine what Elise had in mind. Whatever it was—she just hoped it wasn't embarrassing!

"Prepare for your first Glitter Girl Challenge," Elise said. She giggled. "Come to breakfast tomorrow with peanut butter face masks. And roll your hair with pickles!"

"You've got to be kidding!" Mary-Kate cried.

"What's the matter, Mary-Kate?" Elise asked. "Don't you like peanut butter?"

"Sure!" Mary-Kate said. "On a cracker—not my face!"

Ashley grabbed the peanut butter. "Oh, lighten up, Mary-Kate!" she said. "All this stuff is just goofy fun!"

"Okay, okay," Mary-Kate said. She grabbed the pickle jar. "I'll do the special challenge this time."

But I don't know if I'll do it again, she thought. *Who knew becoming a Glitter Girl would be so much trouble*!

WIN a MARY-KATE & ASHLEY Ultimate Fan Gift Pack!

Are you an **Ultimate Fan**? Now here's your chance for ultimate fun! Enter today, and you could win a gift pack over-flowing with fabulous treasures—including

- a complete book library of TWO OF A KIND™ and THE NEW ADVENTURES OF MARY-KATE & ASHLEY
- the complete *You're Invited to Mary-Kate & Ashley's* video collection
- a complete CD library
- a year's free membership to *Mary-Kate + Ashley's Fun Club*™
- an autographed photo
- *Mary-Kate & Ashley's Dance Party of the Century* CD-ROM video game
- *The New Adventures of Mary-Kate & Ashley* Game Boy Color
- and much, much more!

Even a personal, ten-minute phone call from Mary-Kate and Ashley themselves!*

*subject to availability

Complete this entry form and send it to:

TWO OF A KIND™ Mary-Kate & Ashley Ultimate Fan Sweepstakes

OFFICIAL RULES:

1. No purchase necessary.

2. To enter complete the official entry form or hand print your name, address, and phone number along with the words "Two of a Kind™ Ultimate Fan Sweepstakes" on a 3 x 5 card and mail to: Two of a Kind™ Ultimate Fan Sweepstakes, c/o Harper Entertainment, Attn: Children's Marketing Department, 10 East 53rd Street, New York, NY 10022, postmarked no later than August 31, 2000. Enter as often as you wish, but each entry must be mailed separately. One entry per envelope. Partially completed, illegible or mechanically reproduced entries will not be accepted. Sponsors are not responsible for lost, late, mutilated, illegible, stolen, postage due, incomplete or misdirected entries. All entries become the property of Dualstar Entertainment Group, Inc, and will not be returned.

3. Sweepstakes open to all legal residents of the United States, who are between the ages of five and fifteen by August 31, 2000, excluding employees and immediate family members of HarperCollins, HarperEntertainment, Warner Bros. Television, Parachute Properties and Parachute Press, Inc., and their respective subsidiaries and affiliates, officers, directors, shareholders, employees, agents, attorneys and other representatives (individually and collectively, "Parachute"), Dualstar Entertainment Group, Inc., Dualstar Publications and their respective subsidiaries and affiliates, officers, directors, shareholders, employees, agents, attorneys and other representatives (individually and collectively, "Dualstar"), and their respective parent companies, affiliates, subsidiaries, advertising, promotion and fulfillment agencies, and the persons with whom each of the above are domiciled. Offer void where prohibited or restricted by law.

4. Odds of winning depend on total number of entries received. All prizes will be awarded. Winners will be randomly drawn on or about September 15, 2000 by Harper Entertainment, whose decisions are final. Potential winners will be notified by mail and potential winners will be required to sign and return an affidavit of eligibility and release of liability within 14 days of notification. Prizes won by minors will be awarded to parent or legal guardian who must sign and return all required legal documents. By acceptance of their prize, winners consent to the use of their names, photographs, likeness, and person information by HarperCollins, Parachute, Dualstar, and for publicity and promotional purposes without further compensation except where prohibited.

5.a) One (1) Grand Prize Winner wins a Mary-Kate & Ashley Ultimate Fan Gift Pack, consisting of the following: A complete TWO OF A KIND™ book library, a complete THE NEW ADVENTURES OF MARY-KATE & ASHLEY book library, My Mary-Kate & Ashley Mood Diary, a complete *You're Invited to Mary-Kate & Ashley's* video library, *Passport to Paris*, and *Billboard Dad* videos, a complete Mary-Kate & Ashley CD library, a Mary-Kate & Ashley *Friends of Barbie* doll, a *The New Adventures of Mary-Kate & Ashley* and *Mary-Kate & Ashley's Dance Party of the Century* video game, a year's free membership in *Mary-Kate + Ashley's Fun Club*™, an autographed photograph of Mary-Kate & Ashley, a Mary-Kate & Ashley Sunblock, and a 10-minute phone call from Mary-Kate & Ashley (subject to availability).

b) Ten(10) First Prize Winners win set of the TWO OF A KIND DIARIES, autographed by Mary-Kate & Ashley.

6. Only one prize will be awarded per individual, family, or household. Prizes are non-transferable and cannot be sold or redeemed for cash. No cash substitute is available. Any federal, state or local taxes are the responsibility of the winner. Sponsor may substitute prize of equal or greater value if necessary due to availability.

7. Additional terms: By participating, entrants agree a)to the official rules and decisions of the judges which will be final in all respects; and b) to release, discharge and hold harmless HarperCollins, HarperEntertainment, Warner Bros. Television, Parachute, Dualstar, and their affiliates, subsidiaries and advertising and promotion agencies from and against any and all liability or damages associated with acceptance, use or misuse of any prize received in this sweepstakes.

8. To obtain the name of the winners, please send your request and a self-addressed stamped envelope (excluding residents of Vermont and Washington) to Two of a Kind™ Ultimate Fan Sweepstakes, c/o Harper Entertainment, 10 East 53rd Street, New York, NY 10022 by October 30, 2000.

Double the fashion!
Double the fun!

with Mary-Kate & Ashley Fashion Dolls

Ride with Mary-Kate

Dance with Ashley

Join their slumber party

In Stores Now!

outta-site!
marykateandashley.com
Register Now

DUALSTAR
CONSUMER PRODUCTS

Mary-Kate & Ashley Invite You

To Russia With Love

SUMMER CRUISE: JUNE 25 - JULY 2, 2000

Welcome aboard an awesome cruise vacation to parts
of the world you've only read about. Join Mary-Kate & Ashley
as they explore Finland, Sweden, Estonia and even Russia!
It all begins with a visit to our website at
www.sailwiththestars.com or have your parents call
Sail With The Stars at **805-778-1611**, M-F **9:00 am - 5:00 pm** PST.

Adventures for a Summer. Memories for a Lifetime.

outta-site!
marykateandashley.com
Register Now

Listen To Us!

Greatest Hits

Ballet Party™

Brother For Sale™

I Am The Cute One™

Sleepover Party™

Birthday Party™

*Mary-Kate & Ashley's
CDs and Cassettes
Available Now Wherever
Music is Sold*

Lightyear
Entertainment

DUALSTAR
RECORDS

Distributed
in the
U.S. by
wea

TMs & ©℗2000 Dualstar Records.

Outta-site!
marykateandashley.com
Register Now

TM & © 2000 Dualstar Entertainment Group Inc.

Check out
the Reading Room on
marykateandashley.com
for an exclusive
online chapter preview
of our upcoming book!

DUALSTAR
ONLINE